PHOENIX - F.E.A.R.

Rafael A. Marti

authorHOUSE®

AuthorHouse™
1663 Liberty Drive
Bloomington, IN 47403
www.authorhouse.com
Phone: 833-262-8899

Visit the author's website at www.rafaelamarti.com

Published by AuthorHouse 05/10/2023

ISBN: 979-8-8230-0822-8 (sc)
ISBN: 979-8-8230-0820-4 (hc)
ISBN: 979-8-8230-0821-1 (e)

Library of Congress Control Number: 2023908920

Print information available on the last page.

This book is printed on acid-free paper.

CONTENTS

DEDICATION

For my beloved daughter, Nina Caitlin. You are the reason that I wake up full of hope in the mornings and sleep soundly during the nights. I couldn't ask for a more perfect angel to grace me with the privilege of being her father. Out of all the titles I've held in my life, Soldier, US Army Veteran, Corrections Officer, Operations Coordinator, CEO, Author, none are more prized by me than the one you bestowed upon me when you call me "Dadda."

IN MEMORIAM

Of my dear brother, Alexi, Sr., your infectious laughter, and fun-loving attitude made life an exciting adventure; my loving uncle, Serafin "Junior," your humor and caring are sorely missed. Enjoy paradise alongside of our other dearly departed loved ones. Also, in loving memory of my unborn child, Nina Caitlin's Twin, who did not make it to full term. Dada loves you and misses you even though I never had the blessing of meeting you.

DISCLAIMER

The characters and events portrayed in this book are purely works of fiction. Any resemblance to any real person, whether living or deceased, or any event is merely coincidental. For Mature Audiences. Adult and racist language, sexual and violent scenarios.

PROLOGUE

Life has a way of either working itself out or coming around full circle. Five years have passed since the congressional hearings on the attempts of Nathan Christopher Styles' life. He is currently on the run for his life once again. He's uncertain if he is close to another psychotic break or if the Grim Reaper has finally come to collect on its previously failed attempts. As he hurries down the streets, he discreetly scans his surroundings to make sure that he's not being followed. Suddenly his cellphone rings.

"Mr. Style's you have one hour...tic, toc, tic toc...." then silence.

Vanessa Del Rio hasn't been this terrified since she was held at gunpoint over five years ago when the rogue elements of several government agencies used her as bait to lure out her beloved Nathan in an attempt to ambush him and kill him. Once again, she is being held against her will. Once again, she is being used as bait for the same purpose. Similar yet different circumstances with a complete set of different players.

CHAPTER 1
WOLF IN SHEEP'S CLOTHING

ALL HAIL THE FOUNDER OF F.E.A.R.?

It's a bright and sunny, Spring Day in Philadelphia, Pennsylvania and a crowd is beginning to form on the grounds of City Hall. Most of the people are there to hear the charismatic speaker, Johnathan Lane, announce his bid for candidacy of President of The United States of America. Others are simply curious passersby who have stopped to see why such a large crowd is beginning to form and why the massive media presence is camped out at such an iconic site.

The Media begins broadcasting as they await Mr. Lane's arrival.

"...Johnathan Lane has been said to be the founder of the movement known as Freedom Empowered Active Resistance also known as F.E.A.R., a controversial group of extreme radical separatists..."

"There is no proof that Mr. Lane is connected with..."

"He is just a politician who appears to resonate with approximately forty percent of the American People and his message is captivating the hearts of more and more people..."

As the Media Circus ensues, a white limousine, with a police escort and private security SUVs, pulls up Broad

Street and temporarily parks near the South Entrance of the majestic City Hall Building. The police escort and the private security contractors get out of their respective vehicles and begin radio communications with their counterparts on the North Entrance of City Hall.

"Mr. Lane, you are secure. You may exit the vehicle," says the chauffer/bodyguard as he opens the limousine's door.

"Thank you, Ludwig. I can make my way to the podium from here."

As Johnathan Lane approaches the platform where the podium stands the ever-increasing crowd erupts in applause and cheers. It's as if he were a cult of personality. A modern-day Messiah to most of the crowd gathered there.

"THERE'S NOTHING TO FEAR BUT, (F.E.A.R.) ITSELF" – PRESIDENT F.D.R.

As he pacifies the crowd with a wave of his hands, he approaches the microphone and begins to speak.

"Thank you! Thank you! You are all too kind."

"We love you Mr. Lane," shout random people from the crowd.

"I love all of you too! Now first and foremost I'd like to thank The Lord and Reverend Thomas Magill for his benediction and introduction. Let's give him a hearty round of applause!"

The crowd goes wild applauding, hooting and hollering.

"Thank you! Thank you! You're all too kind. Now if you could all please calm down, I want to get to the heart of the matter."

Silence falls across the area as those gathered there wait with anticipation for their newfound leader to address them.

"For far too long our government has been failing us. They have been trying to force us to accept their radical, socialist agenda and have even kowtowed to their *Woke Movement* and the political correctness. They want us to believe that God makes mistakes and that your gender is not what God made you but, whatever you choose it too be! I say, enough is enough! No longer should our decent, God-fearing citizens be exposed to the abominations of the Devil! No more non-sense! That is why today, I am announcing my candidacy for President of The United States of America! I am counting on you to donate to my campaign and give all you can so, that together we can defeat the corruption of our family values and restore this Country to the greatness God always destined it to have! Remember, God loves a cheerful giver!"

"You're a killer! *Huff!* You're a Warrior! *Puff!* What makes the grass grow? *Huff!* Blood makes the grass grow!" Nathan Christopher Styles lies on his workout bench and uses motivational self-talk that he used when he was on active duty in the US Army.

"Hey GI Joe, take a break before those weights break you," says Vanessa Del Rio his live-in girlfriend. They've been dating for five years and decided to cohabitate two years into their relationship. Theirs is a well-rounded and healthy romance.

"Just one more rep, love," Nathan replies.

Nathan finishes his workout, sits up on his workout bench and is greeted by his lover's soft, tender lips kissing his own. She grabs him by the hand escorts him from their home gym to the shower, where they both proceed to get undressed. They turn on the shower and its steam is nothing compared to the heat emanating from the embrace and kisses of the two enthusiastic lovers. Nathan softly kisses Vanessa on her lips and gently continues kissing her body as he makes his way down her voluptuous curves. Vanessa moans and sighs with each passion filled kiss and begins to beg him to penetrate her. Nathan works his way back up her body neither lover interested in the cascading water that beats on them. He enters her and he feels as though he is experiencing a slight touch of heaven. She lets out a loud moan of pure exquisite delight, grabs and pulls on his hair as he rhythmically thrusts in and out of her. Her fingernails make their way to his back, and she proceeds to dig them into his flesh in ecstasy. The water once very warm begins to cool down as the lovers each climax just in time before the water gets cold.

In City Hall the Mayor is glad that the political rally has ended and that the crowd has dissipated. Mayor Dante Jones is a moderate politician with liberal leanings and is quite adept in the field of the political sciences. He does not approve of billionaires like Johnathan Lane trying to buy their way into the sacred trust of government so that they can amplify their power over the people. It's bad enough that he's been stalling real estate deals in North Philadelphia between Mr. Lane's Foundation and the city because, he believes that it would displace the poor and marginalized individuals who live in North Philly. He wonders how long the City Solicitor, Anne Marie Pacheco, can hold off Mr. Lane's Team of Attorneys. His thoughts are interrupted by his secretary, Joleen Smythe, on the intercom.

"Mayor Jones, you have a call on line three. It sounds like you should take this," she says.

"Thank you, Joleen. I'll take it in my office," he responds.

"Hello, this is Mayor Jones…"

"Mr. Mayor, you don't know us but soon you and your precious city will…" then silence.

CHAPTER 2
WRECKLESS ABANDON

DON'T TAKE LIFE TOO SERIOUSLY YOU'LL NEVER GET OUT OF IT ALIVE

It's evening and a few days have passed since Johnathan Lane announced his candidacy for the highest office in the land. Nathan and Vanessa had seen the news coverage but, did not focus on it much. They are two lovers who are living in the moment and very much enjoying each other's company. Tonight, they plan to paint the town red as the old cliché goes.

"Hey sexy, you almost done in the bathroom? I really need to go," Vanessa inquires.

"Just about, give me a minute…"

"If you don't hurry it up mister you're going to be in trouble."

"You promise," he flirts as he inquires.

"Just hurry!"

"Okay, okay. I'm coming out. It's all yours."

"Finally!" she jokes as she rushes into the bathroom and closes the door behind her.

Brayden Thomas is at a warehouse in the Washington Avenue Factory District located in the Hawthorne and Bella Vista neighborhoods of South Philly. He is surrounded by a group of men and women who share his vision for the future of America.

"Listen up everyone! We started our mission when Johnathan Lane announced his bid for President but, we still have a lot more to do before we accomplish our objective!" he declares. "Tonight, I want John's group to go to the Northside and teach those inside-out niggers, those Spics, that they are not welcomed in our fair city! Make an example of one of them so that they know that this city, hell this Country belongs to F.E.A.R.!"

The crowd goes wild hooting and hollering in agreement. As Brayden vanishes from their midst the group disperses. John grabs a bunch of his goons, and they board a burgundy van headed North on I-95.

"I want this done by the numbers," John briefs his people. "We don't get caught, no one is left behind and if any o' you gets caught you don't spill the beans about the rest of us. We don't want Mr. Thomas to get angry. Got it?"

"Got it!" the group responds in unison as the van continues on its' trajectory to North Philadelphia.

North Philly in a poor and majorly minority residential neighborhood a group of masked individuals roam the streets with bad intentions. Jeremy Vasquez is making his way home from the bus stop on Roosevelt Boulevard after working a double at a restaurant in Northeast Philly. As he walks, minding his own business, with his headphones on listening to music, he turns onto his neighborhood street where he is greeted by the mask wearing group.

"Well, well! What do we have here? Are you one of them Spics or are you a Nigger?"

"I think he's a mix of both," chimes in another member of the group.

Jeremy takes off his headphones and his ear catches the racist insults. He tries to ignore them and passes by a few members of the group without incident. As he continues walking, he realizes that he is now surrounded by the masked cowards. One member of the group strikes him with a steel pipe on the back of the head. Jeremy falls to the ground and the vicious mob proceeds to punch, kick and hit him with foreign objects until his nearly unconscious body is left bruised, bloodied and battered on the sidewalk.

"That ought to teach you, boy! F.E.A.R. is your new

normal," shouts the alpha of the group as he rallies his goons and run off.

It isn't until the wee hours of the morning that the police doing a routine patrol find Jeremy's nearly lifeless body on the streets. They radio for an ambulance and rush him to the hospital.

After the nightclubbing and after-hours clubs Nathan and Vanessa return to their home a little inebriated yet none the worse for wear. They walk, slightly stumbling, to their bedroom where they proceed to take each other's clothes off as they kiss. Vanessa begins to caress his body with her tongue as she works her way down his slim but toned physique. As she drops to her knees, she engulfs his member in her mouth. Nathan gently grabs the back of her head and guides her as he runs his fingers through her hair. Unable to contain his arousal he gingerly raises her up and turns her around, kisses the back of her neck as he enters her from behind and begins to thrust. With every thrust he builds up speed and momentum. Vanessa moans and screams in delight as she clings to the top of their dresser. She can't control herself any longer and climaxes just at the same time as he does. They disengage and collapse on the bed next to them in a sweaty, yet completely satisfied, heap of naked bodies. They glance at each other as they try to catch their breath and begin to giggle.

"That was intense," she pants.

"Yeah, it was divine, my love," he replies.

As they cuddle in bed, Nathan turns on the television and they capture the tail-end of a news story.

"...where he lies on life-support. The police have not released a statement as of this moment..."

"Oh my God! What's going on in this city? It seems like there are more and more people ending up on life-support or in the morgue...," Nathan cries.

"Isn't this like the fourth or fifth person to end up in a similar state in the past few days?" Vanessa asks quite uncertain of the exact number of victims.

"Do you think this has anything to do with?... Nah...It can't be," Nathan thinks it's his paranoid-schizophrenia which he thought he had under control is causing him to jump to conclusions.

"What? What are you thinking?" she asks, her curiosity piqued.

"Well, it seems like ever since Johnathan Lane announced his candidacy for the presidency in this city the violent assaults against Hispanics are climbing," he responds not quite sure of his analysis.

"Well, it has been rumored that he has links to that radical, separatist group…" Vanessa interjects.

"You mean the Freedom Empowered Active Resistance group?"

"Yes, the Media calls them F.E.A.R."

"If they indeed are tied to this string of violent attacks then they are certainly living up to their acronym. People appear to be becoming increasingly afraid."

"You can solve the city's problems later. Let's get some sleep," Vanessa jokingly mocks him.

"Alright. Goodnight, babe."

"Goodnight handsome."

As the two exhausted lovers slip off to slumberland, Nathan's last thought is wondering if he's onto something.

IN THE WORLD OF THE BLIND THE ONE-EYED MAN IS KING

Nathan lies sleeping, Vanessa by his side, what should be peaceful sleep has turned to nightmarish visions. He relives the traumatic incidents of five years ago when rogue agents of several government agencies tried killing him while using his lover as a hostage.

"Come out where we can see you Mr. Styles or she gets it!" yells the mysterious figure who is cloaked by the shadows as he holds an Uzi against Vanessa's head. Nathan steps into the light and is rapidly gunned down.

"Argh! *Huff! Puff!*" Nathan awakens with a scream and his body jolts upright waking Vanessa.

"What's wrong, lover? Is everything alright?" Vanessa asks as she tries to reassure him that he is safe and that he just had a nightmare.

"I…just…had a bad dream," he responds trying to downplay the latest episode of his post-traumatic stress disorder.

With the sunrise dawns a new day and Mayor Dante Jones aims to get to the bottom of the mysterious phone call and the reports of the numerous attacks against minorities that he received last week. He came early into City Hall to try to get a jump on the matter. He calls his secretary on the intercom.

"Joleen, please call a cabinet meeting in the situation room."

"Yes Mayor Jones, right away."

Within minutes the cabinet assembles at city hall's situation room. Mayor Jones tells Chief of Police, Robert Dewey, to patch him through to the Department of Homeland Security in a video conference call.

"This is The Governor's Office of The Department of Homeland Security Southeast Regional Office, Intergovernmental Affairs, Pennsylvania Commission on Latino Affairs, Jose Rodriguez speaking. How can we help?"

"This is Mayor Dante Jones of Philadelphia. We would like to coordinate with federal, state, county, and municipal government agencies on a matter of serious concern against our Latino Community. There has been a spike in what appear to be terroristic hate crimes against this demographic in my city and I want to get to the bottom of who is or are responsible for this. The latest victim was a young man in North Philadelphia, Orphaned, working double shifts to support his little sister and attending Thomas Jefferson University on a scholarship to become a nurse. The kid has no priors and was doing his best to get out of a difficult situation, poverty, to better his life for himself and his seven years old sister. He was brutally assaulted by a group. We believe that the group was the Freedom Empowered Active Resistance or as we call them 'F.E.A.R.' We are working on establishing if there is a connection between these terroristic hate crimes and the group's radical agenda."

"We will begin coordinating our efforts with other government agencies and your office right away," Jose responds.

Johnathan Lane slams the phone on his desk frustrated.

"How dare the mayor not take my call! What could be more important than my plans to revitalized North Philadelphia?" he thinks.

His thoughts drift back to the simpler times of his childhood and the Philadelphia in which he grew up in. Like many people, he idealizes the past and only remembers the good times. If he were to travel back in time, he would know that the more things change the more they stay the same. His reminiscing is interrupted by the ring of his encrypted cellphone.

"This is Johnathan Lane," he answers.

"I think we're close to accomplishing our objective."

"Keep my posted," Johnathan says as he hangs up.

Vanessa is off to work as a Psychiatrist at the Department of Veterans Affairs Medical Center located at Woodland Avenue in Philadelphia. She landed this job shortly after graduating from college and has left the job as bartender behind far in the rearview mirror of her life. Nathan takes his morning medications and chases them down with a swig of black and sweet coffee. He turns on the television and decides to watch the morning news.

"...There are still no arrests in the assault of 20-year-old Jeremy Vasquez which has left the young, orphaned college student on life support fighting for his life. Police are asking for any leads regarding this incident. This is the latest in what appears to be an ever-increasing string of hate crimes against the Latino Community. If you have any information regarding this or any of the incidents police urge you to call in anonymously 555-NO-CRIME..." the News Anchorwoman continues with her reporting but, Nathan has stopped listening.

Her voice has become distant, faint background noise

as his mind kicks into overdrive. While in the United States Army, Nathan Christopher Styles, was a Green Beret, Special Forces but although cross-trained in every one of his A-Team's specialties, his primary specialty was Intelligence. He viewed the world differently than most and his paranoia only accentuated his analytical abilities while his schizophrenia made it difficult to trust his own assessments.

He begins to wonder if the rise of violent attacks against the Latino Community are tied to the speeches full of diatribe against minorities specifically Latinos from Presidential Candidate Johnathan Lane's political rallies throughout the country. It's been years since he has kept in touch with his former colleagues from the teams but, he decides to reach out to Ariel Benitez, nonetheless. He picks up his cellphone, finds his name on the contacts and punches it. The phone seems to ring forever, when finally on the other end an all too familiar voice answers.

"Hello, Styles. Long time no speak. How have you been?" responds Ariel.

"Hi Benitez. I apologize for not staying in touch much…"

"I know, I know. Life has a tendency of getting in the way."

"Umm...yeah...it's still no excuse..." Nathan comments embarrassed.

"Water under the bridge. No worries. To what do I owe the pleasure of this call?"

"I just wanted to see how you're doing?" Nathan says half-truthfully.

The conversation continues for a few minutes, and they say their goodbyes and hang-up. Nathan is relieved that Benitez and his bond has endured. Yet, he feels bad about not being completely honest with his ol' friend. His mind reels with possible scenarios of how the conversation could have turned out. He is afraid that his schizophrenia is skewing his judgement. Perhaps he's jumping to conclusions or is his intuition on point regarding Johnathan Lane. As he wrestles with this, he also battles with why he didn't ask Benitez the questions he wanted to ask. His mind in turmoil he decides that he will go to the hospital and check on Jeremy Vasquez. Perhaps there he can find some clues and regain some sort of clarity on the situation. His anxiety attacks him out of nowhere one of the many joys of his disorders. He breathes deep and takes a clonazepam pill and chews it hoping that the anti-anxiety drug will quickly do its job and calm him down. As for his racing thoughts induced by the stress fueled schizophrenic assault, he tries to shake it off, temporarily being successful at quieting the voices in his head.

CHAPTER 3
THE DON QUIXOTE QUEST

HERE IN LIES THE RUB

Jeremy Vasquez is still in the Intensive Care Unit of Temple University Hospital. The ventilator was just taken off. He is no longer on life support but, remains in critical condition. The doctors are pleased with how rapidly he is recovering. He has been slipping in and out of consciousness. The police detectives have been in and out of his hospital room trying to get as much information as possible regarding the assault. Sensing that Jeremy's tired they decide to follow some leads and leave the patient to rest and recover.

Scant minutes after the detectives depart, Nathan Christopher arrives at Jeremy's ICU Room under the guise of being his longtime friend. He's lucky Jeremy is still conscious. He introduces himself and asks Jeremy if he wouldn't mind answering a few questions.

"Are you another cop?" Jeremy asks weakly.

"No, I'm not. I just want to get to the bottom of the attacks against our Latino Community and I was hoping you could shed some light on your assailants."

"With a name like Nathan Christopher Styles you don't sound Latino at all..."

"My mother was Puerto Rican and therefore so am I. I recall her stories of the mistreatment of our people when her father migrated from the Island to the mainland in order to work the farms and try to make a better life for his family. In this day and age, I would have thought that Latinos would have been accepted by now but…"

"You're an idealistic fool to believe that and thanks for the history lesson. Ugh! Huh! However, My parents were killed by a white supremacist when I just turned eighteen and the police weren't able to do anything about it. Just like they're just going through the motions with my situation…"

"Well, I want to help."

"What are you some kind of vigilante?"

"No. I'm a US Army Veteran. I took an oath when I enlisted to defend this Country against all enemies foreign and domestic. That oath has no expiration date…"

"So, you're a hero with a Messiah Complex. What are you going to be able to do?"

"I'm no hero. I'm going to do what the police can't or won't do. I'm going to take the war to them."

Jeremy briefs Nathan as best as he can. Just as Nathan is about to depart Jeremy stops him cold in his tracks by uttering these words,

"Ugh, I forgot to mention this to the police but, they also said that this city and this Country belong to F.E.A.R."

⚜

In the Warehouse/Factory District of South Philly, Brayden Thomas sits in his office contemplating his next move. His cellphone rings interrupting his train of thought and he answers it.

"Hello?"

"Hello Mr. Thomas. I hope I did not call at an inopportune time."

"Not at all Ma'am. What can I do for you?"

"There appears that the Vasquez kid had a visitor this afternoon other than the usual police detectives," says the mysterious woman an in irritated tone.

"I hope that this person isn't what's got you perturbed?"

"Well, he might be problematic. It appears that his visitor was none other than Nathan Styles."

"Should this name ring a bell for me?"

"Five years ago, he aided the Federal Bureau of Investigations in exposing and apprehending rogue agents of several government agencies who were trying to silence him after they experimented on him. It was all over the news media outlets. A Congressional Hearing was even held on the conspiracy. I'm surprised you are not familiar with the matter."

"Heck, I can't remember what I ate for dinner last night, let alone this incident you're talking about. What's he doing visiting the Spic in the hospital for?"

"I don't think they have a history. As a matter of fact, I find it very unlikely. I want you to send some men to gather intel on him. Find his weaknesses and any personal attachments he may have; they should come in handy to leverage against him should he become a nuisance."

"Yes, Ma'am. I will send some of my best people to trail him."

"I just texted you his picture and the information that I have on him."

"I got it. Should we do anything about the Vasquez kid?"

"Silence him, permanently. Don't fail me now. You wouldn't want 'you know who' to come down hard on you."

"Understood, Ma'am. F.E.A.R. won't let you down."

"You better not, for your sake," she says as she hangs up on him.

Brayden Thomas doesn't intimidate easily yet; he fears what she and her partner are capable of doing to him and F.E.A.R. should he or his people upset them.

In City Hall Mayor Dante Jones convenes another meeting with his cabinet and leaders of various governmental offices in the Situation Room with Homeland Security on video conference to discuss any progress on the terroristic rise of hate crimes in Philadelphia.

"So, where do we stand Chief Dewey?"

Robert Dewey has been Chief of Police since before Mayor Jones was sworn in. His loyalty is to law and order and his sworn oath to protect and serve.

"Honorable Mayor, we are still not anywhere near linking these increasing attacks against the Latino Community to the Freedom Empowered Active Resistance a.k.a. F.E.A.R. Perhaps Mr. Rodriguez from Homeland Security can shed some light onto the situation?"

"Mayor Jones, Chief Dewey, Cabinet Members,

Esteemed Leaders of The Joint Task Force, Homeland Security is in the process of trying to infiltrate F.E.A.R. with undercover agents and attempting to uncover potential moles in that organization. As of this moment it is an ongoing operation, and I can't share any more info than that than you all already know. Upon a successful incursion of our agents into F.E.A.R. we will be able to coordinate efforts to bring them to justice if they are responsible for the attacks."

Vanessa Del Rio is exhausted from a full day's work at the Philadelphia Veterans Hospital. She logs off her work computer and makes her way out of the complex. As she is making her way out, she pulls out her personal cellphone from her purse and dials Nathan.

"Hey sexy! How was work?" Nathan answers.

"Good handsome," she replies.

"Great! I've got to talk to you when you get home."

"Is everything alright? You sound excited yet different, honey."

"I'm okay. Just get here as soon as you can. I don't want to talk about this over the phone," Nathan states.

Vanessa has been Nathan's lover and confidant for a

little over five years, and she's come to know him and when he's acting a little paranoid. She hopes that he is not still ruminating about the conversation they had during pillow talk yesterday at the wee hours of the morning. She knows he doesn't take injustice lightly and may want to do something about the attacks they heard on the news. For once in her life, she prays that her intuition is wrong and that she's just reading into things too much. She walks through the parking lot, gets in her car and proceeds to go home.

Twenty minutes pass and she enters her abode which she shares with the love of her life, Nathan Christopher Styles. She's curious by what she discovers in the living room. There's Nathan taping newspaper articles on a whiteboard, making annotations and connecting the articles with strings of yarn.

"Hey lover, whatcha doin'?"

"I am trying to connect the dots. I know F.E.A.R. is behind the attacks and…"

"How did you come to this conclusion, hun?" she asks concerned that her boyfriend might be going off the deep end again.

"I visited Jeremy Vasquez in the ICU today…"

"You did what?!"

"Hear me out. Like I said, I visited Jeremy today and he confirmed it for me. Now I'm trying to figure out where they are operating out of and give them a taste of their own medicine."

"Are you crazy! If Jeremy knows it was them then I'm sure he told the police. Let them handle this..."

"We both know that the police will only arrest them if they have enough evidence for the District Attorney to make a conviction stick. Besides Jeremy forgot to tell the police."

Nathan rambles on his theory that he believes that presidential candidate Johnathan Lane is behind F.E.A.R. and that he's got to find a way to prove it or should he ascend to the presidency this country is screwed. As he rambles on Vanessa believes that his paranoid-schizophrenia is starting to consume him again as she fights back the tears that well up in her eyes.

ARE THEY WINDMILLS OR DRAGONS?

A solitary, beautiful, young woman walks into Temple University Hospital asking for the room of Jeremy Vasquez. She claims to be his girlfriend as she sobs and walks past the ICU Nurses' Station and into his room. Jeremy is sleeping as his body tries to heal from the brutal assault, he endured just a couple of nights ago. She visits for a while and then pulls out a syringe full of a natural cocktail that will gradually cause him to go into cardiac arrest without leaving a trace and injects it into his IV. She walks out of the hospital room and exits the building.

An hour later, Jeremy's vitals begin to go wild. The nurses respond to the alarms emanating from his room.

"He's going into cardiac arrest, code blue! Code blue! Bring the crash cart, stat!"

As the nurses and doctors try to resuscitate Jeremy, he flatlines and the realization that there is nothing they can do to revive him begins to set in. The exhausted medical team are frustrated with their failed attempts and the doctor says, "I'm calling it, time at approximately twenty, forty-four hours, Mr. Vasquez has expired."

Vanessa has listened to Nathan's theories ad nauseum and tries to reality check him with no success. She believes that she should give him and some space and decides to take a shower and call it a night. Nathan is frustrated that Vanessa cannot seem to see the connections he's made of F.E.A.R. to Presidential Candidate Johnathan Lane. He decides that discretion is the better part of valor and gives her some space. He sits on the couch and turns on the TV to a twenty-four-hour news channel. They are showing highlights of Johnathan Lane's latest rally in Texas.

"...we must make our Country God's Country again! These Latinos come to our shores or across our border with their Santeria, Voodoo and their version of Catholicism which are an abomination to the true Christian God! They come and corrupt our family values, impregnate our daughters and abandon them with their half-breed bastard children or worse yet force them to get abortions killing the unborn! They lack morals! They don't want to learn English or become Americans! They just want to steal our women! Steal our jobs! They want to live off the government programs created by the Socialists! I say it's time we fight back before we become the minorities in our own Country! I vow to make changes for our benefit..." Nathan's heard enough and powers off the TV.

"What a racist moron! If he only knew that our founding fathers intended this Country to be a melting pot and for there to be a separation of church and state," he thinks aloud still fuming from what he's just witnessed on the TV.

Vanessa enters the living room to say goodnight but hearing Nathan's outburst at the turned off TV she grows more concerned about the state of his mental health and becomes afraid. She opts to do a quick U-Turn to the bedroom and instead of going to bed, gets ready to go out with her girlfriends. She believes that Nathan is losing it again and needs time away from the drama and stress.

North Philadelphia or North Philly as it is commonly known is not the most ideal of neighborhoods. To some people it is considered the ghetto, but to its residents the poor and minorities, mainly Latinos, who live here it is a community. They live in rowhomes, look out for each other and frequently shop at the corner bodega. The bodega is a mini supermarket called *De Todo Un Poco* translated from the Spanish to mean *A Little Bit Of Everything* it is owned by Raul Gonzales a fixture in the once vibrant and thriving neighborhood. This particular section of North Philly has seen its best years behind it, with inflation and unemployment for the unskilled or under educated rising, these factors have had a negative impact on the residents here. There's a large section of elderly who reside here and Raul often extends credit to those who have fallen on these hard times in an effort to ease their socio-economic pain and make sure they have what they need to simply survive with some sort of dignity. Though most of North Philly may appear to be in disarray this neighborhood polices itself and are content in doing so. They've seen difficult times in their history, but Raul comforts them and reminds them that these times too shall pass.

Ironically, it's one of the neighborhoods that the Presidential Candidate Johnathan Lane's Foundation wants to revitalize. The same area that the City Solicitor Anne Marie Pacheco is trying to block Mr. Lane from purchasing in an effort to keep the poor, elderly and predominantly Latino Community from being displaced.

Raul Gonzales has been a pillar of the community since the 1970's when he was a young man and inherited the bodega from his late father. Around every Thanksgiving he distributes free meals with a small turkey to the elderly and less fortunate in the neighborhood while absorbing the costs. Some would call it a foolish business practice but to him it's a way of giving back and caring for his community. He has been an unlicensed therapist to the youth in the 'hood talking them out of lives of crimes or drugs. Respected and adored by the community, he has been a very vocal inspiration to the people speaking out against gentrification. He certainly has not gone unnoticed by the Johnathan Lane Foundation.

On this particular evening, he is closing up shop for the day. He's sweeping up the sidewalk in front of his beloved bodega. The youthful neighbors walk past him and engage in conversation with him. He takes his time to hear them out and wishes them a good night and proceeds to lock the bodega down as they slowly walk away.

Suddenly, SUV's and vans come screeching around the corner tossing Molotov cocktails at the bodega and neighboring row homes. It is a terroristic, arsonist attack organized by F.E.A.R. to produce shock and awe. Raul shouts at the attackers as he races to the nearby homes in an attempt to rescue the residents before they burn to death. One of the young women who was previously talking with Raul Gonzales calls nine-one-one. The cowardly arsonists are long gone as the fires rage more out of control. Raul has managed to rescue several elderly residents before collapsing on the floor due to excessive smoke inhalation. In the distance one can hear the firetruck, ambulance and police sirens.

CHAPTER 4
BE HE HERO
OR MARTYR

HELL HATH, NO FURY

The inferno rages on in the once peaceful neighborhood in North Philly. The smoke billows from the burning bodega and nearby row homes like demons escaping from hell. The stench of the burning buildings permeates the air threatening to suffocate anyone who gets too close to them, or the unfortunate souls still trapped in their blazing homes. The firetrucks, ambulances and police cars come to a screeching halt and begin their coordinated efforts to do damage control and rescue people. Two EMTs rush to the side of Raul's lifeless body on the sidewalk and proceed to administer CPR in an effort to revive him, as other EMTs deal with the remaining victims. The police proceed to escort the people who gathered from the neighborhood behind the crime scene tape which their fellow officers have put up, while the firemen battle the flames with their water hoses as they simultaneously rescue the remaining victims from their burning homes. Police officers gather statements from the eyewitnesses and attempt to methodically put the pieces of the puzzle together.

The neighbors cry as they see their homes once engulfed by fire reduced to ash, cinder and rubble.

EMT's bring out a body-bag for Raul's corpse causing the onlookers to wail in grief and despair. Their longtime friend and advocate has perished due to apparent smoke inhalation. Some fear that their hopes along with their livelihood have been reduced to rubble not unlike some of their homes. Now the question remains; will he be remembered as a hero or a martyr?

From across the Roosevelt Boulevard a solitary figure watches through binoculars the controlled chaos and grins before walking to the nearby gas station and leaving in the backseat of a black sedan.

The passenger in the black sedan calls her partner and benefactor.

"Hello, lover. It's happening just as you said it would. The residents are dismayed and afraid now that their leader has died."

"Strike the shepherd and the sheep will scatter," he replies.

"I love it when you get all philosophical and quote the Bible."

"There'll be time for foreplay later. Now onto the next part of the plan. We have to ensure that no one else rises up in his place to cause us any further problems or delays."

"I have a very close eye on a potential threat but, I think I can handle it."

"Good. Have Mr. Thomas and his group disrupt any marches or protests over the death of that inside-out nigger that just died. I will see you soon."

"Okay, lover."

In City Hall, Police Chief Dewey just got off of the phone with the police captain on the scene in North Philadelphia. He turns to the Mayor, the members of the Mayor's Cabinet, the leaders of the Joint Task Force and Jose Rodriguez from Homeland Security who is still on video conference with them and says, "Honorable Mayor, Ladies and Gentlemen it appears as if the situation has gotten worse and it's escalating."

He briefs them on the report he just received from the police captain on the scene in North Philly.

Mayor Dante Jones, enraged, tells them, "We need to stop this escalation and show whoever is responsible that hell hath no fury like our Justice Department! I will not tolerate any more assaults against my constituents or my beloved city!"

"Well, you heard the Mayor. Let's get to work!" Chief Dewey says as he tries to rally the troops.

TO BASK IN THE AFTERGLOW

The members of F.E.A.R. have gathered at their makeshift headquarters in South Philadelphia. They're hooting and shouting victoriously as they watch the news on the television and basking in the afterglow of their most recent attempt to purge the city of what they view as the vermin to society. They await to be addressed by their leader, Brayden Thomas.

Within minutes their fearless leader emerges from his office and commences to deliver his address to them.

"Good night, ladies and gentlemen. I'm proud of the work you did tonight. You did good! Now, I just got off the phone with our benefactors and they want to be certain that that inside-out nigger, Raul Gonzales, does not become a martyr to the scum we are trying to rid this beautiful city from. We need to be on alert for any marches in his memory...better yet, I want a group of you to disrupt his funeral. A dog like him doesn't deserve a decent Christian Funeral or Burial. I want to strike fear into any of his friends' hearts and scare them before they even think of organizing. All we want them to know is F.E.A.R.!"

The crowd goes wild with chants of, "No Peace For The Spics!"

Brayden Thomas waits for his posse's chants to die down and then thanks them again and dismisses them.

It's nearly five o'clock in the morning, and Vanessa crawls into bed after a night of celebrating, careful not to awaken Nathan Christopher. Little does she know that he woke up when he heard the front door open as she made her way into the apartment. He just opted to feign sleep and wait for her to fall asleep before getting up. When she awakens, they will have to discuss her whereabouts last night and why she neglected to answer his calls throughout the night.

He decides to slither out of bed and tiptoe out of the bedroom, turns on the TV and heads to the kitchen to prepare a cup of coffee. The twenty-four-hour news channel is on, and he hears about the horrific incident that transpired last night in North Philadelphia.

"What the hell is happening to this city? It's utter

and complete chaos out there and I have a gut feeling that this F.E.A.R. group is responsible," he thinks to himself.

He decides to call his ol' US Army Special Forces Teammate and friend, Ariel Benitez, again.

"Hello Styles, to what do I owe the pleasure of you calling me twice in as many days?"

"Hi Benitez, did I call at a bad time?"

"Never, brother. I always have time for you."

"Same here, brother. I apologize for not being completely honest with you when I called you the other day. True, I wanted to see how you were doing, but I also had another reason for my call."

"Don't worry about it. Shoot. How can I help you?"

"It involves the incidents that are occurring in the city where I live. I'm sure you've seen or have heard of it on the news."

"Yeah, Philly is going to shit. How does this involve you?"

"Remember our oath of enlistment? The part about protecting this country from all enemies foreign and domestic?"

"Of course."

"Well, the people responsible for these terrible attacks

are domestic terrorists and it hits close to home for me aside from the oath we took which has no expiration date."

"How so?"

"They are targeting the Hispanic Community in the city that I live in and I'm part Hispanic. Heck, I have family that are Hispanic that live in this city. I don't want anything bad to happen to them."

"Gotcha, how can I help?"

"I need you to ferret out the leader or leaders of F.E.A.R. Are you up for an unsanctioned black op? We could get in trouble or killed?"

"Sure! When has that stopped us before. Eat healthy, stay fit, die anyway. I've got your six. So, what's your plan?"

Nathan discusses his plan with Ariel and Ariel agrees to head to Philadelphia. Just as they conclude their hours-long conversation, Vanessa enters the kitchen.

"You're up?"

"Yeah, I couldn't sleep much."

"Where were you last night? I called you several times and you didn't answer."

"I was out with the girls, and I couldn't hear the phone ring because the music was so loud."

"I didn't even know that you were heading out."

"What are you, my father? Do I look like a kid to you? Do I have to tell you my every move?"

"No, but you didn't even say goodbye."

"Well, you were yelling at the TV that was turned off! I was scared to approach you!"

"I was upset at what I saw on the news and had just turned off the TV."

"I think that you are obsessing over everything and that's not good for your mental health! Can we shelve this discussion for some other time? I must get ready! I have things to do!"

Nathan realizes she's upset and begins to wonder whether she is right. Is his schizo-affective disorder and anxiety getting the best of him? Is he spiraling out of control?

CHAPTER 5
AM I MY OWN
WORST ENEMY?

CHAOS AND CONFUSION

Days go by and the funeral for Raul Gonzales arrives. Nathan goes alone to One Cathedral Basilica of Saints Peter and Paul which is located in Center City within walking distance of City Hall where a Funeral Mass is being held for Raul Gonzales, the much beloved, late advocate for the neighborhood in North Philadelphia which is being target for gentrification by the Presidential Candidate Johnathan Lane's Foundation. Nathan notices the large crowd of people entering the majestic cathedral but, he cannot take in the architectural wonder erected before him. He's too much in his head over the fact that the love of his life, Vanessa, hasn't spoken to him since he upset her a few days ago. He can't help but wonder how he can make amends. Perhaps she's right about him starting to lose it again, he wonders. His heart aches and the heartache is only compounded by the solemn Mass which begins to take place as he enters the Holy Sanctuary. Due to the crowd size, he takes a seat in one of the back pews. It's as if the entire city, people of every race and religious creed, have come to pay their respects for this fallen hometown hero.

The Archbishop of Philadelphia is presiding over the

Funeral Mass. Nathan hears only parts of the liturgy but, he's far too much in his head, doubting himself and wondering if he's invested himself in trying to uncover the recent hate-crimes maybe a little too much at the expense of his relationship. He's always been an independent, strong-willed individual. He never let anyone in but, somehow Vanessa crept into his heart like a ninja, stealthily. Has he become too dependent on her and her love, he wonders. Has the once mighty warrior been domesticated? Back when he was a Special Operator with the US Army, he used to compartmentalize his emotions more efficiently and effectively. It wasn't until, the experimental vaccines were administered to him causing him to suffer a psychotic break and develop paranoid-schizophrenia and generalized anxiety disorders, that he began to doubt himself and question his judgement.

People within the cathedral are sobbing, crying and paying their respects to the fallen hometown hero. However, to Nathan it appears as if he's only catching glimpses of all the ceremony and actions. He is too lost in thought. Suddenly, the cast bronze doors to the cathedral burst open and a group of people yell and throw teargas cannisters into the holy sanctuary. The cannisters explode emitting the noxious teargas all over the inside of the cathedral. The perpetrators escape and close the doors behind them. The mass of people in the cathedral are frightened, panicking, coughing, tearing, choking on the teargas. They begin to stampede towards the front exit in an effort to escape. Chaos and confusion erupt among the crowd. Nathan instinctively tries to help the people get out of the smoke-filled building. The group is too large to control and the tidal wave of people push him outside where a small contingent of F.E.A.R. awaits them all. The members of F.E.A.R. are armed with stun-guns, bats, chains and other weapons.

WE NEED A HERO!

Nathan stumbles out of the cathedral with the massive group of people surrounding him. He does not see the domestic terrorists that await them as they rush out of the building. Quickly his battle-honed situational awareness kicks in. He begins to scan the crowd looking for potential threats and in rapid succession he finds his targets. They are wearing ski-masks and brandishing an assortment of weapons which they're using on the people who are attempting to escape the teargas filled cathedral.

Nathan makes a beeline for his nearest target who is beating on an elderly Hispanic couple with a steel pipe. As the assailant raises the pipe one more time, Nathan blocks the strike and lands a palm strike on the perp's chin causing his head to go back. As the member of F.E.A.R. falls back, Nathan mounts him and begins pounding on him while trying to gain any valuable intelligence he can. Another member of F.E.A.R. rushes to his comrade's aid approaching Nathan from what he believes to be Nathan's blind spot. Nathan sees him ready to hit him with a baseball bat and deftly rolls out of the way. As he rolls out of harm's way, he instinctively kicks the assailant in the knee with such force causing it to shatter. Nathan then springs up an delivers an uppercut knocking out the domestic terrorist. He scans his surroundings and locates his next target. As he begins to descend on the predator turned prey another F.E.A.R. member shoots him with a taser in the back.

Nathan goes down convulsing from the electrical currents coursing through his body. He fights to remain conscious but is shot again by two more stun-guns. As his vision begins to fade to black, he sees the members of F.E.A.R. scramble and he hears police sirens approaching in the distance. Before losing consciousness, he wonders what will happen next and whether the intel he was able to extract from the perp via force was actionable?

CHAPTER 6
COME TO YOUR SENSES

LAW AND ORDER

The police arrive on the scene and radio in for ambulances to join them. The aftermath of the terrorist attack has the victims reeling, confused, hurt and angered as to how some people would dare desecrate this solemn moment held for the late, Raul Gonzales, the once advocate and deceased hometown hero. The EMTs arrive and start tending to the wounded Nathan Christopher, unconscious, among them. The victims give their statements to the police of the horrible incident that just transpired. The police captain calls in the incident report to, Robert Dewey, the Police Chief for the City of Philadelphia.

Robert Dewey is a career law enforcement officer never one to give into politics. He's a no nonsense, fit, dedicated former Marine. He's just received the report of the attack that occurred at One Cathedral Basilica of Saints of Peter and Paul and is fuming. He leaves the precinct he was inspecting and heads for City Hall while enroute he calls, Dante Jones, the current Mayor of Philadelphia and his current boss. He briefs the Mayor on what's happened near City Hall.

"They are becoming bolder and bolder!" exclaims the Mayor into the phone.

"They're also becoming more reckless," begins to explain Chief Dewey. "We could use this to our advantage. A sigma male confronted them and took the battle to them, I'm told."

"Have you identified the hero?"

"I'm told that it was Nathan Christopher Styles, former US Army Special Forces, Green Beret."

"Nathan Christopher Styles, why does that name ring a bell?"

"Approximately five years ago, he exposed rogue agents in the alphabet soup agencies and helped bring them to justice."

"Hmmm…That's right! I remember hearing of him now. He could be useful to us. Where is he at this moment?"

"He was found unconscious onsite and was transported to Temple University Hospital for evaluation and observation. I was told it took three shots from tasers to bring him down but, he managed to inflict some damage on a couple of the domestic terrorists before they subdued him."

"He's of great interest to me. Don't let anyone talk

to him. I want us to get his statement here once he's discharged."

"I'll go retrieve him now."

"Good, I will convene the cabinet, the joint task force leaders in the Situation Room and get, Jose Rodriguez, from Homeland Security on video conference. We have to determine how their attempts at infiltrating and locating F.E.A.R. are going."

"Roger that, Mayor! I will see you soon with Mr. Styles in tow."

Vanessa is busy at work wrapping up a psychiatric session with one of her patients at the Veterans Affairs Hospital in Philadelphia. As the session expires and her patient leaves, she decides to take her lunch break. She's in two minds. She is still upset about Nathan's interrogation of her whereabouts a few nights ago and concerned about his recent demeanor. Is he starting to let his paranoid-schizophrenia and anxiety disorders get the best of him? Is he relapsing? These thoughts run through her head as she enters a breakroom to eat her packed lunch.

She glances at the television which is broadcasting a twenty-four-hour news channel.

"…attack on One Cathedral Basilica of Saints Peter and Paul near the heart of Center City, Philadelphia has left several wounded who have been transported to nearby hospitals…"

Intuitively, she fears that Nathan Christopher's involved in this mess. She thinks she recalls him saying that he was going to pay his respects to the fallen hometown hero at that location. Worried, she tries to call him but, he isn't answering his cell phone.

"If he's okay, he's going to wish he wasn't when I get ahold of him. How could he leave me worried about him like this? Oh God, please let him be okay," she thinks to herself.

She's an ocean of contradicting emotions inside and she hopes her shift ends soon so that she can check on her beloved.

The members of the assault party return to F.E.A.R. Headquarters scared out of their minds. They wonder if the police have followed them, even though they took alternate routes and checked their backs to make certain that they didn't have any tails. They begin talking amongst themselves wondering who in the hell was the beast that counterattacked them. Just then, Brayden Thomas walks out of his office, after watching the breaking news reports, and approaches the returning crusaders.

"Welcome back, my avenging angels," Brayden exclaims as he approaches the assault team.

As he gets closer, he notices that his assault team appears frightened and are tending to two wounded personnel. His demeanor changes. He inquires as to what happened and is quickly briefed by the assault team's field leader. Brayden assures them all that they will get their vengeance on their assailant. He excuses himself and heads up to his office to await the right moment to make a phone call to one of his benefactors.

Chief Dewey walks into the emergency room where Nathan Christopher Styles is beginning to regain consciousness.

"Hello Mr. Styles, my name is Robert Dewey. I'm the Chief of Police for the City of Philadelphia."

"Am I in trouble?," he asks weakly, as his mind is still in a fog.

"No, sir. The Mayor wants me to take your statement at City Hall."

"Why City Hall?"

"Mayor Jones considers you an asset that could assist us during the ongoing crisis."

"An asset? Uhg!"

"Yes, given your history, the Mayor believes that you can be of value to our current investigation."

Nathan's phone rings and he sees it's Vanessa calling him. He excuses himself from the conversation and answers the call. He greets her and asks to table their disagreement until he returns home. He informs her that he's being discharged and going to meet with the Mayor regarding the incident which he was involved in. Vanessa is upset and asks him to stay out of it. He informs her that he doesn't have a choice in the matter, says "See you, soon.", and hangs up on her.

THE DIME DROPS

Brayden Thomas receives a return call from the benefactor he left a message for earlier. He answers the call, is given the details he requested and agrees to the nefarious plot concocted by his superiors. The call is ended, and he heads out of his office to brief and rally the troops.

⁓⁂⁓

Mayor Dante Jones eagerly awaits Nathan Christopher Styles' arrival as he is briefed in detail by members of his cabinet, the leaders of the Joint Task Force and his Homeland Security Liaison.

"…infiltrating their organization and trying to get not only enough evidence and the root but the leader and/or leaders as well," explained Jose Rodriguez of Homeland Security.

"Our Joint Task Force in Operation 'Awakens The Dreamer' is making plenty of headway but, I fear that at the rate that F.E.A.R. is escalating things it may be too little too late," counters the Mayor.

"Never fear ladies and gents, Chief Dewey is here, and I come bearing a gift."

"Tell me you did do as you were instructed," Mayor Jones inquires.

"Don't I always."

"With all due respect, if this operation is too succeed

we need to be kept in the loop on everything that's going on," Rodriguez chimes in.

"Keep your shirt on, Jose! I just happen to have in the other room none other than Nathan Christopher Styles the hero who fought back against the members of F.E.A.R. during their latest assault."

Vanessa is infuriated as she logs off for the day and heads into the parking lot to retrieve her vehicle. Suddenly, two women with guns hidden in their jacket pockets come up behind her and tell her to get in the black SUV or get shot. Vanessa is frightened and follows orders. She blames herself for not heeding Nathan's warnings and training on situational awareness but, she blames Nathan more for she is afraid that this involves him somehow.

Nathan is patiently waiting in a separate room to be debriefed and briefed on how he could be of service to the Mayor when he answers his phone.

"Is this Nathan Christopher Styles?," asks the individual on the other end of the call.

"This is he," Nathan responds recognizing the fact that the phone number is blocked from his phone's caller ID and that whoever is speaking is utilizing a voice modulator to disguise his or her voice.

"We have Vanessa Del Rio in our care and if you ever want to see her alive again, you will do exactly as you're told."

His heart drops and he reluctantly agrees to their demands.

Chief Dewey, proud of his accomplishment in securing Mr. Styles, leaves the situation room and goes to get City Hall's honored guest. Much to his chagrin, Nathan is not waiting for him patiently in the room. He quickly scours the massive complex only to realize that he will have to inform the Mayor and the leaders of the Joint Task Force that Nathan Christopher Styles has flown the coop.

CHAPTER 7
LUCK BE A LADY
TONIGHT

AGAINST THE CLOCK

Life has a way of either working itself out or coming around full circle. Five years have passed since the congressional hearings on the attempts of Nathan Christopher Styles' life. He is currently on the run for his life once again. He's uncertain if he is close to another psychotic break or if the Grim Reaper has finally come to collect on its previously failed attempts. As he hurries down the streets, he discreetly scans his surroundings to make sure that he's not being followed. Suddenly his cellphone rings.

"Mr. Style's you have one hour...tic, toc, tic toc...." then silence.

Vanessa Del Rio hasn't been this terrified since she was held at gunpoint over five years ago when the rogue elements of several government agencies used her as bait to lure out her beloved Nathan in an attempt to ambush him and kill him. Once again, she is being held against her will. Once again, she is being used as bait for the same purpose. Similar yet different circumstances with a complete set of different players.

⋘⋙

Mayor Dante Jones is beyond pissed-off and blows his top in front of the members of his cabinet and the leaders of the Joint Task Force.

"Where in the Hell did Styles disappear to," he yells at Chief Dewey.

"I don't know, Mayor. But I will put out an APB on our person of interest right away."

"You do that! I want Styles found and I want him as of yesterday!"

⋘⋙

Nathan is under duress and the strain of his and Vanessa's current predicament threatens to bring him to the breaking point of another psychotic meltdown. He's worried about the wellbeing and life of his lover and of his own. Just as things look hopeless, his phone rings and he answers it.

"Hey Styles! Where are you off to in such a hurry?"

"Hi Benitez, What the fuck took you so long?"

"I've been tracking you since you left the hospital. Care to fill me in on what's going on?"

"Everything is FUBAR!" *(Fucked Up Beyond All Recognition)*

"How so?"

"These bastards have Vanessa hostage and told me to come alone or else they'll kill her!"

"How you end up eating shit-burgers so often astounds me. No worries, I've got your six."

"Well, don't get spotted or they'll kill her!"

"Roger That! I'm a ghost and you should be too. Don't go in there without a plan. That Rambo shit only works in the movies, remember that."

"Roger, Out."

SNAKE EYES

Luck seems to be running out for Nathan, but he doesn't believe in luck. He's a cold, tactical, killing machine. Unfortunately, his psyche is on the verge of a breakdown. As he fights the voices in his head threatening to drive him insane, he wonders if he can rely on what he sees before him. Is reality real or is his psychosis beginning to emerge? He battles the inner demons that threaten to overwhelm him. His situational awareness is diminished. His mind is foggy, and his judgement is impaired. His anxiety is through the roof as he tries to formulate a plan of action on the fly.

As he approaches the address provided to him by the ominous voice on the phone earlier, he realizes that he is in the warehouse district in South Philadelphia. He tries to move stealthily and he notices a group of ten sentries guarding the entrance into the building. He decides that alone he only has one recourse. That one recourse is to feign surrender and take out the guards by hand, confiscate their assault rifles and breach the building. He sure hopes that Ariel Benitez is close by to provide some sort of support.

"Here goes nothing," he thinks as he approaches the group with his hands up in the air. For a man who doesn't like gambling he was definitely taking a huge risk. He could be shot to death on sight but he prays that the universe will conspire with him and his plan will work.

"Hello! I'm Nathan Christopher Styles," he shouts as he approaches. "I was told to come here by myself and surrender!"

The guards look stunned at his arrival and comment

amongst themselves, "Will you look at this dumb fuck? Little does he know what's in store for him when the boss gets ahold of him."

His ploy is working. He's not dead yet, he thinks as he continues his approach. The group of sentries with their assault rifles trained on him begin to surround him. In a succession of deft moves, Nathan grabs the barrel of one assault rifle and uses the same rifle to butt-stroke the guy wielding it causing the domestic terrorist to fall back unconscious. The other members of the group are under strict orders not to kill him so they refrain from firing on him.

Nathan then kills another member by delivering a lethal palm strike to the individuals nose causing the cartilage of the nose to break and enter the perp's frontal lobe. As the late terrorist collapses, Nathan thinks to himself two down eight to go. He blocks their blows and counterattacks breaking the jaw of another guard. A six feet five inches tall goon who looks like he weighed approximately two hundred and ninety pounds of pure muscles spears him to the ground and mounts him. Nathan, the wind knocked out of him, instinctively grabs the assailant's throat with both hands and using all of his strength rips out the attacker's Adam's apple.

Nathan doesn't stop until the hulking man-beast on top of him goes limp.

Styles is fending off his attackers and quickly shoves the dead weight off of him and springs to his feet. He thinks of Vanessa and worries that by killing all the guards he could get her killed in retaliation. As he is about to surrender, Ariel Benitez from a close by rooftop snipes the remaining six sentries. "Boo! Motherfuckers!" Benitez says to himself as he fires the shots from the sniper rifle he got from his Philadelphia safehouse.

"Mayor Jones, we just received reports of shots fired in the warehouse district in South Philly!"

"That's where our intel tells us that F.E.A.R. is headquartered," reports Jose Rodriguez from Homeland Security.

"Okay, time for this Joint Task Force to Awaken The Dreamer and go live," commands the Mayor.

The leaders of the various organizations that comprise the Joint Task Force call in their subordinates on the ground and initiate the operation.

Nathan breaches the building. As he enters, he is greeted by more goons of F.E.A.R. He starts to fight them using Krav Maga, Brazilian Jiu-Jitsu, Army Combatives, Kenpo and everything in his fighting arsenal. He is making great strides as he mows down several F.E.A.R. members, but not getting much intel on the whereabouts of his beloved Vanessa. The voices in his head are persistent in trying to cause him to go into a psychotic tailspin. Disoriented he momentarily drops his guard and is struck in the back of the head by the butt of a rifle knocking him out cold. As he falls the members of F.E.A.R. are on top off him punching and stomping on him as others use rope to restrain him and drag his near lifeless body away to their leader.

CHAPTER 8
AWAKENS THE
DREAMER

ET TU?

Nathan's near lifeless body is brought before Brayden Thomas. Brayden instructs his loyal followers to secure Mr. Styles to a chair which has a spotlight overhead. Shortly after Nathan is tied to the chair, Brayden instructs one of his cronies to throw water on him in order to awaken him. Nathan begins to come to and realizes his predicament.

"Ugh! Where is she? What have you done to Vanessa? If you so much as have hurt a hair on her head, I'll kill all of you!"

"Hush, Mr. Styles! You are hardly in the position to ask questions or make any viable threats now. Wouldn't you agree?"

"You filthy bigot! Just wait until I get my hands around your throat..."

"Now, now, Mr. Styles or should I call you Nathan? Nathan, I understand you're half Spic. In other words you're a mutt, half of the superior race and half of you is an inside-out nigger. We can't have half breeds like you trying to stop our mission..."

"And what exactly is your mission? To remake this country into what would have been Hitler's Paradise?"

"Close but we have to start somewhere and why not

start by ridding it of the Spics, then the Niggers, the Jews, and so on and so forth…"

"Your plan is doomed to fail you dumb motherfucker! The United States of America is a melting-pot!"

"The United States of America, ha! Not very united in this day and age now, is it?"

"If the majority of Philly has united because of the atrocities you and your domestic terrorists have committed; what makes you think that the majority of the country won't follow suit?"

"Easy, most people have the attention span of goldfish. They rally behind a cause and then fall off after a few weeks. They are sheep and lack conviction. If things don't impact them directly they quickly forget about what's happening until it's their turn to suffer the same fate as those persecuted before them."

"You don't give people enough credit…"

"And you give them too much! Why is it that only one percent of the population are willing to serve in the armed forces regardless of the sacrifices they must make; while the majority of the people just stay enjoying the comforts of peace? Getting fat, dumb and lazy…"

"Leave it to bigoted, little minded individuals like

you to distort the facts. People care and when it comes to times of crisis, they unite…"

"That may have been true at one time but, look at society now. They only care about immediate gratification. Long gone are the days of selfless service and sacrifice."

"Well, I'm here and I have a purpose and that is to rid this city of the plague that is F.E.A.R."

"You are a dreamer, aren't you? F.E.A.R. is much larger than you can possibly imagine. And to show you just how large we are allow me to introduce you to its founder…"

No sooner does Brayden Thomas utter these words than the current Presidential Candidate Johnathan Lane appear with Vanessa in a collar with a thin chain attached to her neck. At the sight of Vanessa being lead like a dog on a leash Nathan loses his composure and shouts,

"You piece of shit! Let go of her now! God so help me, when I get free of these constraints I will kill you all!"

"Calm down, Nathan! She's here of her own free will and accord. Isn't that right my little sex slave?"

AWAKEN TO A NIGHTMARE

Nathan can't believe what Johnathan Lane has just told him. He's in disbelief. Perhaps Vanessa is too frightened to speak out. Given their current predicament he doesn't blame her. All the while Nathan's been attempting to free himself from the ropes that restrain him. He's grateful that the dimwits who tied him up were not sailors because, they couldn't tie a proper knot if their life depended on it. Still the image of Vanessa on a leash and the words of Johnathan torment him and momentarily stunned by the optics of it all he's forgotten to free himself. Instead he calls the presidential candidate a liar.

"If I'm lying, why do you think we let you live this long? I wanted to break you before she kills you!"

With those words said, Johnathan yanks on Vanessa's leash and she draws close to him and passionately kisses him in the mouth. Nathan is very much on the verge of psychosis and feels completely betrayed and almost defeated. Nathan struggles to keep it together and cries out,

"Tell me this isn't true! Tell me you are being forced to do this Vanessa!"

"Sorry not sorry love! I met Johnathan during a

lecture while I was in college and was smitten with him instantly."

"So, you've been cheating on me this whole time?!"

Nathan is beside himself as his already broken heart sinks. He can't still fathom that his whole relationship has been nothing but a lie. His psyche is being held together by bubble gum. He feels as though he is going to lose his grip on reality and as he notices this part of him welcomes the abyss. If this is his reality, he wants no part of it.

"Oh, grow up Nathan! Nothing lasts forever!"

"But he's a hate spewing bigot!"

"He's also great in the sack and will be the most powerful man in the world when he becomes President of The United States of America."

"I thought you loved me?"

"I did. Until I met Johnathan. He turned my entire world view on its head. Why should I settle for a broken soldier when I can have it all?"

Johnathan instructs Brayden to supply Vanessa with a gun. Vanessa blinded by loyalty to this cult of personality takes the weapon. By sheer willpower Nathan tries to snap out of it and manages to discreetly free himself from the ropes that bound him. Vanessa takes aim at Nathan's chest and Nathan leaps forward before she fires hitting her hands as she fires. The errant bullet strikes Johnathan Lane's head causing his brain-matter to explode out of the side. Johnathan crumples to the ground and Vanessa distraught drops the gun to the floor. Before Nathan can grab it, the Joint Task Force storms the building.

"This is a raid! Drop your weapons! Nobody moves," yell members of the Joint Task Force.

The Joint Task Force sweep the compound and arrest everyone in sight. As Nathan is being escorted out in flexicuffs, Chief Robert Dewey recognizes him and asks the joint task force operative to remove the cuffs and release him into his custody.

EPILOGUE

News reports from all over the country broadcast the aftermath of Philadelphia's Mayor and The Joint Task Force's successful raid against The Freedom Empowered Active Resistance also known as F.E.A.R. Nathan has been cooperative in the investigation and the District Attorney has agreed not to press charges on him for killing the members of F.E.A.R. as an act of self-defense. Just as Nathan is about to leave the police precinct Chief Dewey advises him not to leave the country until after the trial of Vanessa and the members of F.E.A.R.

Nathan Christopher thinks to himself about his brother-in-arms Ariel Benitez when his cell phone rings. He answers the call and the person on the other side says,

"Boo!" and hangs up.

He knows Benitez is well now and starts to play the entire scenario over in his head. The past five years, the betrayal and the aftermath of it all. He thinks back to his late mother's words of wisdom. "Some people are just placed in your life to teach you a lesson." The lesson this once domesticated warrior has learned is:

"Once a Soldier, Always a Soldier!"
THE END

Printed in the United States
by Baker & Taylor Publisher Services